Shoe

AMY LAURENS

OTHER WORKS

SANCTUARY SERIES

Where Shadows Rise
Through Roads Between
When Worlds Collide

KADITEOS SERIES

How Not To Acquire A Castle

STORM FOXES SERIES

A Fox of Storms and Starlight
A Stag Of Hope And Memory

SHORTER WORKS

April Showers
Bones Of The Sea
Darkness And Good
Dreaming Of Forests
Rush Job
Trust Issues

NON-FICTION

How To Write Dogs
How To Theme
How To Create Cultures
How To Create Life
How To Map

Find other works by the author at
www.amylaurens.com

Shoe

INKLET #65

AMY LAURENS

Inkprint PRESS

www.inkprintpress.com

Print ISBN: 978-1-925825-67-1
eBook ISBN: 9798201147709

www.inkprintpress.com

National Library of Australia Cataloguing-in-Publication Data
Laurens, Amy 1985 –
Shoe
36 p.
ISBN: 978-1-925825-67-1
Inkprint Press, Canberra, Australia
1. Fiction—Horror 2. Fiction—Fantasy—Dark Fantasy
3. Fiction—Short Stories

First Print Edition: September 2021
Cover photo © Susy Noda via Pixabay
Cover design © Inkprint Press
Interior art © Amy Laurens

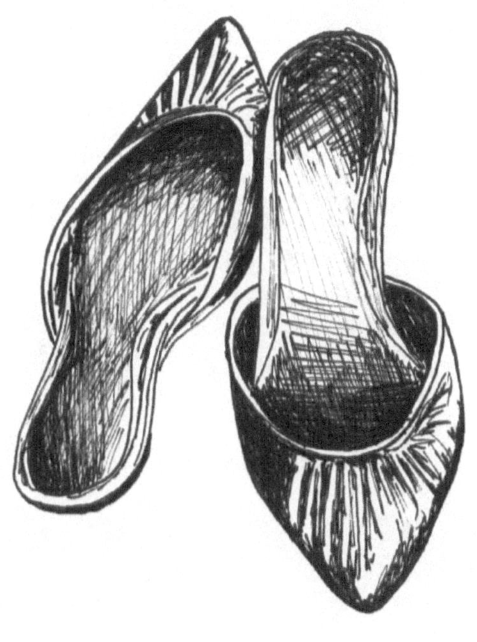

SHOE

THE SHOE LAY BY THE ROAD, WAITING. Someone would pick it up. Someone always did.

Jenna halted. A shoe lay in her way. *A* shoe, just one, lying on its side. Strange.

She peered at it. Black, pointy toe with pleats in the leather... It looked exactly like Carina's shoes, the ones Jenna had been envying for the last month. Gorgeous shoes. She'd tried them on once when Carina was out.

But this was only one shoe. She couldn't wear one. She turned away.

Tink.

Jenna looked back. The shoe stood upright—and it stared at her forlornly.

Wind gusted down the street and the shoe rocked on its slender heel. Jenna knelt in front of it. It looked so vulnerable…

The wind puffed again, and Jenna decided. She scooped the shoe up. It didn't matter that it was pair-less. She couldn't leave it out here alone.

Jenna set the shoe on the table.

She'd polished it until it gleamed, and set against the mahogany table it created a pleasant still-life.

Pleasing…

But the shoe looked empty.

Jenna drummed her fingers on her chin, wondering if it was stupid to try on a pair-less shoe.

The light bulb overhead flickered and the shoe seemed to wink at her. "I'll keep your secret," it might have said.

Jenna grinned.

She kicked off her sneakers and wriggled out of her socks. She slipped her foot into the shoe, giggling—then frowned.

It was too big.

But only just. She might be able to manage... Jenna stood, and twitched in surprise as the soft leather contracted. She must have been mistaken. The shoe fit perfectly.

I wonder what it looks like, she thought.

Unwilling to remove the shoe, she tottered to her bedroom and posed in front of her mirror.

She tilted her head, examining her foot's reflection.

The clouds drifted and a shaft of sunlight shot through her window, pinning the shoe in its beam.

Jenna gasped. Not only did the shoe fit her perfectly, it was *stunning*. Her ankles had never looked so slender, and the height of the heel showed off her calf to its full advantage.

Hmm. I wonder. She had a dress, a slinky black number with a swishy skirt that she'd had on that time she'd tried Carina's shoes…

She pulled it out of the wardrobe, slipped into it, and stood before the mirror again.

And frowned.

The mirror was too small.

Carina has a full-length mirror.

The thought came out of nowhere, but Jenna smiled happily. *So she does.*

She trotted down the hall to her sister's bedroom. She threw her head

up, sucked in her stomach, and admir-
ed her reflection.

The clouds shifted again, and a
gleam in the mirror caught Jenna's eye.

Carina's shoes.

It wasn't like Carina to leave her
things lying around.

And yet there were the shoes,
sprawling out from under the bed-
spread.

Jenna looked down at the shoe on
her foot, then back at Carina's pair. It
wasn't even like she'd have to try *both*
of them on...

An image of Carina, hands on hips,
popped into her mind. "If you don't
stop going through my stuff whenever
I'm not here I'm going to get a lock for
my door."

Jenna gave a guilty shiver—but she
had never *hurt* anything. Carina *always*
overreacted.

Jenna pressed her fingers against
her lips. The lights flickered, and Cari-

na's shoes winked at her. She nodded. "Okay. Just one of you."

She dropped to the floor and pulled the left shoe on, wriggling her toes in delight. She scrambled to her feet and posed again. Perfect!

Her right foot began to tap.

She frowned. When did she decide to do that?

Oh. Probably about the same time she'd begun to hear that wildly infectious music, thrumming past her ears like blood, rushing and roaring and making her want to dance.

She whirled, giggling as her dress fanned out. The music sped up and Jenna twirled again.

But the room was too small.

It wasn't made for dancing.

She skipped out to the lounge room.

Much better. This time when she twirled, there were no walls to impede the perfect flare of her skirt.

Impulsively, she reached up and pulled out her hair-band. She shook her head, dark waves cascading over her shoulders.

She spun again, clapping her hands as her hair flared out like her skirt.

People should see this.

Jenna flung open the front door, raced down the path, and onto the street.

A deep belly-laugh surged up and she clapped in time to the music. Her feet seemed to have taken on a life of their own, and she tapped and twisted and kicked, the black shoes inky shadows in the evening light.

One shadow slightly darker than the other.

Jenna kicked again and again, lifting her legs high to mark the rhythm.

A car approached.

She noticed it out of the corner of her eye, but it didn't really matter. She was dancing, the driver would see that.

Surely no one could help but be infected the moment they heard the music—and they'd hear it as soon as they came near, for it was loud and strong.

She giggled and ducked in mock curtsey to the on-coming vehicle. Its roar blended into the song with deep percussion undertones that tugged at Jenna's stomach. She hugged herself.

"Come!" she yelled. "Come and join!"

The car obeyed, racing closer as though it couldn't wait to dance with Jenna and the wild music.

Jenna spread her arms, welcoming the car. She reached out to hug it, wanting to whip it up around so that it too could feel the weightlessness of the dance.

Her laugh changed to a scream as the car hit her.

Her body fell limply to the road.

She might have just been sleeping.

Her right foot twitched.
The shoe fell off.
It lay by the road, waiting. Someone would pick it up. Someone always did.

THE MAKING OF
SHOE

This, one of the first short stories I ever wrote and certainly one of the first I ever sold for real, actual, up-front money, was inspired by *The Red Shoes*, a fairy tale by Hans Christian Anderson that had intrigued me for no particular reason I can put my finger on since high school.

In fact, I once did a charcoal A3 illustration of an empty bedroom, footsteps shining on the floor, with an open window—and an open, empty shoebox. I think that was in Year 10, the peak, so far, of my art experiences (though I'm trying to get back into it these days!).

I've also always been fascinated by the shoes that get left on the sides of roads, especially fast freeways. I understand how children's shoes can go astray—cast out the window, perhaps, by a slightly wayward child, or lost out the door after an emergency roadside stop due to emergency nappy changes or puking or just general Small Person Issues.

But adults shoes?

How does an adult lose a shoe—especially just *one* shoe—on the side of a fast-moving freeway, where it's ill-advised to pull over on the shoulder for anything short of life and death?

Which of course is the answer: obviously these shoes must relate to life and death...

And what if the shoe itself was death, and *wanted* to be left on the roadside so that, virus-like, or like a parasite, it could infect a new host and move on?

After all, there is a species of hookworm that makes infected ants climb to the top of the highest blade of grass and dance like mad so that the sheep (or is it cattle?) that the worm lives out the rest of its life cycle in will eat the ant, and thus the worm.

And we've all seen pictures of *Ophiocordyceps unilateralis*, that horrifying fungal parasite that causes insects to go mad and behave strangely right before they explode with a miniature mushroom blossoming out of their head, the spores flying out to infect the insect's comrades nearby.

Obviously, parasitical shoes are just the Next Logical Step, and apparently Hans Christian Anderson thought so too.

Read more by Amy Laurens!

BONES OF THE SEA

THE MAN—WHOSE NAME IS IRRELEVANT, FOR HE shall soon be dead—wandered down the beach where sand whiter than any he'd seen before swashed between a short, head-high cliff to his left, and the frothing waves of the ocean to his right. Salt filled the air, but below that, something else lingered, and he couldn't quite place his... nose... on what it was.

Of course, the locals were horrified that he was here at all. But he was a Man Of Learning, and was not accustomed to heeding the warnings of people obviously less learned than himself, especially when they spoke tales of a beach that left no trespasser alive.

He'd scoffed. Ridiculous, their legends of a beach where to set one toe on the sand was to seal your own death sentence before the rising of the next full moon.

He was far more interested in analysing the sand, quite literally whiter than any he'd seen before, and thus far resistant to his attempts to decode it. He'd thought a pure variety of quartz before he'd arrived, but upon reaching the beach, pulling into the little deserted cul-de-sac dead end, festoonned with warning signs ('Cursed Beach, Do Not Enter'; 'Beware The Bones Of The Sea'), he'd switched his engine off, opened the car door to the sound of waves and wind through the saltbush, and he'd seen the sharp drop-off down to the sand and had changed his mind to chalk, or maybe gypsum.

But there'd been no tiny fossils his portable microscope could detect, and the sand, whatever it was made from, had failed to fizz under the application of a drop of acid from his little glass vial, so that struck gypsum and chalk from the list of options.

Now, after several hours on the beach to no avail as the hot evening sun seared his hands and the light glinting off the ocean—and, of course, the white sand—blinded him, he'd had enough. He'd run out of fresh water, ideas, and patience all, and was presently hiking back around the cove to his car that glinted silver and tantalising at the far end of the beach, a haven of cool air and fresh water.

Stay. Stay a little while longer.

The salt clung to his skin, filming his lips, the inside of his nose, the back of his throat. Somehow, the ocean smelled sharper here, more concentrated. Briefly, he wondered if that was the source of the townsfolk's rumours; but a higher salt concentration ought to have meant people floated better, drowned less. No. There must simply be a convergence of factors that meant the currents here were particularly treacherous, and indeed, casting his gaze out to the distance horizon, examining the interplay of wave and off-white foam, the cove did indeed seem to be quite swirly, with a few smooth tracts he thought were probably rips.

As ever, folklore had a logical series of explanations behind it.

Just a little longer.

His leather sandal caught on something in the sand.

He stumbled.

That hurt.

Whatever it was, it had poked through the holes in his footwear to stab at his toes.

Glaring, impatient, this nameless victim kicked away some of the strange, defiant white sand—and inhaled sharply.

Once the initial burst of adrenalin subsided—a thing a surprise human skull will inevitably inspire, regardless of one's general composure—it seemed obvious.

Of course. The one thing he hadn't tested for was bone.

So focused on unlocking the mystery of the sand's composition was he that his initial reaction was deep, gleeful satisfaction.

Dawning understanding, however, made him lift his feet, hesitantly at first, shaking the white sand—bone—sand, think of it as sand, it's safer that way—but it's bone, really it's bone, it's all bone, every single grain of it, pure white, sun-bleached bone, spat up from the guts of the ocean the way a predatory owl spits out the bones of its prey, and then his feet were dancing, just like his stomach, as he leapt for the cliff and tried to haul himself up and off the beach because God, oh God, he was standing on bones and only bones, and the skull he'd un covered had been human, and there, just down the beach, that rock wasn't a rock, it was another skull, and oh God, how many people had died here?

He realised the sobbing was his, rasps of panic as he scrabbled at the cliff face that should have been easier to climb than it was, his fingers digging at the rock, skin tearing, sandals scraping for purchase…

Stay.

His back was to the ocean when the freak wave rose, a local tsunami of salt and hunger, and smashed into him.

As it dragged him out to sea, all he felt was cold, so bitter it froze his bones right in his body.

An hour later, as the sun spilled red-orange lifeblood out over the ocean, the ocean spat a skull, bleached-white and grinning, back up onto the beach. A moment later, as the full moon crested over the craggy headland behind, a sternum—*most* of its ribs still attached—joined the skull, followed a moment later by a single scapula.

And as the moon rose, and the ocean swallowed the sun, a whisper began that sounded like the wind… until you realised there was nothing but saltbush for the wind to disturb, and the whispers sounded strangely like a voice, hungry, crooning, and singing.

Feed me.

Feeed mee.

Feeeed meeeeee….

Keep reading! Head to
www.amylaurens.com/books/sanctuary/where-shadows-rise/
to buy your copy now!

ABOUT THE AUTHOR

AMY LAURENS is an Australian author of fantasy fiction for all ages. Luckily, she has never picked up a discarded shoe that didn't belong to someone she already knew—though she concedes that that fact alone does not ensure said shoe is actually safe.

Amy has also written the award-winning portal-fantasy *Sanctuary* series about Edge, a 13-year-old girl forced to move to a small country town because of witness protection (the first book is *Where Shadows Rise*), the humorous fantasy *Kaditeos* series, following newly graduated Evil Overlord Mercury as she attempts to acquire a castle, the young adult series *Storm Foxes*, about love and magic and family in small town Australia, and a whole host of non-fiction.

INKLETS

Collect them all! Released on the 1st and 15th of each month.

INKLET #055
Allure
AMY LAURENS

INKLET #056
The LIES We KNOW
LIANA BROOKS

DOUBLE
INKLET #057
AFTERMATH & Fool Me Once
AMY LAURENS

INKLET #058
Purity
An Age Of Unicorns Story
AMY LAURENS

INKLET #059
Saved
AMY LAURENS

INKLET #060
A Kiss is the Secret
AMY LAURENS

INKLET #061
A Changing Tides Story
Fire Bright
AMY LAURENS

INKLET #062
Hades AND Persephone
LIANA BROOKS

INKLET #063
Just So Long As You're Happy
AMY LAURENS

INKLET #064
Theft Of A Lifetime
LIANA BROOKS

INKLET #065
Shoe
AMY LAURENS

INKLET #066
Published AUTHOR
LIANA BROOKS

DOUBLE ISSUE
INKLET #067
THE REMARKABLE INSIGHT OF JELLYBEANS & Understanding
AMY LAURENS

INKLET #068
Desperate Measures
AMY LAURENS

INKLET #069
Rock-a-bye
LIANA BROOKS

INKLET #070
the Other Carly
AMY LAURENS

INKLET #071
Bs By Bioluminescent light
AMY LAURENS

INKLET #072
Even Villains Grant Wishes
A Heroes & Villains Story
LIANA BROOKS

www.ingramcontent.com/pod-product-compliance
Lightning Source LLC
Chambersburg PA
CBHW030814190726
48285CB00003B/1171